MEG'S FIN/

CW01460930

A NOTE FROM THE AUTHOR;

Megs journey is my first book. It is a very short story of a strong willed persons refusal to accept their destiny, with twists and turns and ends with one final conclusion. It is based loosely on a dream I experienced and I knew I had to bring the story to life.

A reader has described this story of being both 'Disconcerting and emotional'. My subsequent books are longer stories as I have progressed in my writing career and will be available very soon. I Hope you enjoy reading Meg as much as I enjoyed writing it.

MEG'S FINAL JOURNEY

T. A. Marshall

YOUCAXTON
PUBLICATIONS

ISBN 978-1-915972-77-4

Published by YouCaxton Publications 2025

YouCaxton Publications

www.youcaxton.co.uk

For Tara, not only my dear daughter, but my truthful and very honest critic. xx

Contents

CHAPTER 1

SENTENCE

The prognosis was not good. Weeks, maybe a month – that was all. How on earth could this be happening? The consultant carried on speaking but Meg Larkin did not hear much more, except for a couple of words... new pain medication... hospice... The room started to spin, nausea overwhelming Meg's body.

Meg's gran Anna was sat in the seat next to her and grasped Meg's hand tightly and Meg quickly moved it away. Meg tried to stand, to try and get away from the awful situation, but her legs would not move. It was as though she was glued to the chair.

She managed to mumble 'No there must be some mistake, I do not feel unwell, except for the headaches, I feel okay...' she trailed off, her voice unable to function properly.

The consultant shook his head, and her gran now instinctively put her arm around Meg. The room started to spin again, and the familiar feeling of nausea overwhelmed Meg's body once again as the reality of what she had just been told sank in. Anna was now wiping away her own tears. Shock then turned to anger in Megs mind.

'Why me?' she thought.

She then imagined she had said this out loud but was not sure, her mind a merry-go-round. Maybe it was just her subconscious saying it. She had never felt this much out of control. The consultant was looking gravely at her, and she heard him mumble some words about multiple tumours and no treatment. She grasped the painkillers from the desk and hastily left the room, her gran closely following her. She was in a daze, vaguely aware of Anna trying to give words of comfort, all of which did not register; they felt alien to her and did not feel comforting at all. She had just been given a life sentence. A sentence to death which was very close on the horizon.

Meg made it outside, somewhere where she felt she could breathe, her gran following her close behind. She sat on a nearby bench and stared aimlessly into the distance. Anna took a seat next to her but kept silent. Meg noticed this and appreciated it. She needed time to reflect, to think of what her future held. As Meg sat she heard the birds singing on this spring April day and the noise of a cyclist pedalling past. She listened to these noises intently, trying to block out the feelings of dread which were now manifesting themselves in her head. She listened to the hum of traffic from the nearby town centre, the sound of someone's car alarm in the next street. All of these sounds she would usually take for granted. But today, Meg took them all in, enjoying listening to the sounds of a normal day, normality. Something she needed today most of all. Normality it is then, she suddenly realised as she got up.

'Come on gran, let's get going,' she suddenly said, getting up quickly and Anna solemnly accompanied her to the car.

Meg had an independent life which she enjoyed immensely. She had been an only child and tragically lost both parents when she was eleven. Her gran, Anna, had stepped in and became her guardian. Meg had lived with her gran for the rest of her childhood in the same town they both lived in now. After leaving school Meg went on to study journalism. She gained her degree, moved out of her gran's and into her own little house less than a mile away.

Her house was her little safe haven, somewhere she could relax and totally be herself. After university she had acquired a post at Tapton Bros News and had worked there ever since. This was in the heart of the small town and was one of the main hubs of it. Something was always happening in the town, some sort of fundraiser – a fete, a charity event – and so all of these stories and articles kept the little news office alive and thriving. When Meg had first started working there, she felt so full of aspirations and ambition but sadly, as the years passed, her role started to become more mediocre and ordinary to her. As she grew older, she seemed to lack any aspiration or pretension and she seemed to have lost her drive. She felt she had not got the ambition to progress or the will to chase the dream anymore. She was not unhappy in her role; she just felt contented to stay as she was with the normality of it and the regularity.

Meg had a few friends but much preferred her own company. The actual closest friend she had was a work colleague named Sadie. Meg had contemplated on many occasions that this liking for isolation was probably because she was an only child and was so used to being on her own, doing her own thing. She had remained single and felt happy being so. Boyfriends came and went. There had been no one special enough for Meg to want to commit to a full-blown relationship. All the hearts-and-flowers kind of thing, she mused, no, that was not her in the slightest. She smiled to herself as this thought fleetingly passed through her mind. Reflecting on this, she had noticed though, in the past few years that a few of her friends had remarked and some had joked that she might be left on the shelf – but this did not bother her at all; she was content with her single life and she adored it.

Her dear gran, Anna, had played the important part of guider and mentor, and as the years had elapsed, Meg felt herself becoming estranged from her more and more. As well as gardening and crossword puzzles, one of her gran's main interests was in the psychic, afterlife phenomenon. She regularly attended 'meetings' as she called them, but Meg understood they were full-on seances. As a non-believer Meg was sometimes infuriated by this and always tried to divert the conversation when her gran started speaking about it. On those occasions Meg often felt irate with her only remaining family member. But at times like this she had to remind herself that these 'meetings' were probably the most sociable event of the week for her gran and, although

Meg did not agree with it, she had to respect her gran's interests.

Meg had been healthy and well up to six months ago. Then she had started experiencing excruciating headaches and on occasions her vision had been blurred. After seeing doctor after doctor, she was eventually diagnosed with a small brain tumour. She had been told previously that it was harmless as it was but would have to be removed if it got any bigger or her symptoms got any worse. This did worry her at first, but she became very good at denying it and, apart from the headaches, she had no other major symptoms. As time went on, she pushed it out of her mind and she was no longer worried about it. Deep down she thought, the longer she could go without surgery the better. But these things have a habit of creeping up on oneself. And now this last consultation was not good news. Multiple tumours had been found and her condition was now un-operable and, sadly, terminal.

In her gran's car her gran tried to make conversation with Meg.

'Shall I drop you at yours love? Or would you prefer to come to mine for a while?'

The words rang in the silence of the car. Meg did not feel like answering. She eventually pulled her thoughts around to the present and decided she would call in to work and inform her boss she was going to take some time off.

'No, it is fine. Drop me at home, I need to do some things this afternoon.' Meg replied.

Her gran looked quite concerned, but then she smiled.

'If that's what you want to do. I will phone you later on. Don't forget I am at a meeting tonight though, so will not be able to answer my phone.'

How could Meg forget about her gran's little meetings!

'Fine, Gran, I will speak to you afterwards then.'

'Oh, and please do not forget your tablets, dear, and take them regular as the doctor said, to keep the pain at bay.' Anna handed Meg the new prescription.

Meg took the package from her and kissed her gran on the cheek. 'Speak soon, love you,' she said before hurrying through her front door.

CHAPTER 2

DENIAL

Meg glanced at herself in the mirror. Looking a little closer, she thought she looked a little drawn and maybe a little off colour, but after studying the face looking back at her, on the whole she thought she did not look like someone at death's door. She mused to herself light heartedly, a gentle smile emerging on her face. She studied her reflection more, taking in her tall slender body, her little button nose. She admired her long brown curls, which framed a pretty face, her brown eyes matching perfectly with her hair. Same colour as her mother's, she contemplated. In fact it was almost like looking at her younger mother stood there in front of the mirror. This was how she remembered her mother and she was now around the same age too. It was both amazing and astonishing to see – but also quite comforting.

A feeling of heartfelt warmth ran through Meg's body. She could remember her parents well. She was eleven when the tragic accident had occurred, and since then her life had never been the same. She revelled in the memories for a few minutes and remembered the delightful smell of her mother, the musk of her perfume, lilies as she remembered. She always had to have a sniff of these flowers if she saw any. It was a consoling scent, a smell of warmth and love. A slight tear fell from her eye. She wiped it away immediately. She turned from the mirror and thought she needed to get on. Things to do, she grabbed her phone, swallowed a few of the new tablets, called a cab and headed for the office.

Later, Meg wandered into the office in a very confident mood, gone was the bedraggled mess she had been earlier in the day. . She was not going to let anyone feel any sympathy for her; she felt she could not deal with it right now. It was very quiet in the reception area which was quite alarming as usually it was a hustle of voices. She was not looking forward to this task at all but smiled – hiding a million apprehensions. She mooched through the main door, up to her desk which looked very neat and minimalistic, her laptop taking centre stage. She gazed around the room, at the sea of desks, overcrowded, full of family photos, personalised mugs and trinkets in very stark contrast to her own desk. Meg's desk contained no photos of husbands, lovers, children or siblings; it contained just the minimum office stationery. She thought to herself that she had never really noticed this until now and a little sadness engulfed her for a few seconds. She then stood for a minute taking everything in, feeling a little overwhelmed, as this might be the last time, for a while, she was in this environment, an environment that had become usual, regular, maybe even comforting to her. She tried to compose herself in readiness for her meeting with her boss. Breaking her thoughts, Sadie came out of the kitchen area and as soon as she saw Meg, she hurried over to her and hugged her.

'I am so sorry,' she started to say.

But Meg put her hand on Sadie's cheek. 'It is fine, I feel fine, everything is going to be okay.'

Sadie's face showed a slight sadness but then that turned into a weak smile. 'If you say so and you sure you are feeling ok?'

Meg replied, 'Yes totally, not even got a headache today yet, I have got some new tablets please try not to worry.' She placed a hand on Sadie shoulder affectionally.

They were interrupted by their boss. He looked sheepishly at Meg. She realised this straight away and took the lead, not wanting anyone to feel sorry for her.

'Could I have a word please?' she said and he gestured towards his office. Sadie gave her a fleeting look.

Once inside Meg spoke. 'I would like a bit of time off please.' She spoke confidently 'Just until I get myself together, get the pain under control.'

Her boss looked at her in an unusual way, a look she had not seen before. 'Err, yes, you know that is fine Miss Larkin,' he replied. 'Take all the time you want.' He clearly did not know how to handle this situation and Meg noticed he did not give much eye contact, kept his head bowed.

She carried on: 'I have just come over to collect my laptop and a few personal things. As soon as I feel a bit better, I will log on and catch up with my work. Is that ok Mr Tapton?'

Again the man in front of her did not give her any eye contact. He glanced at the wall behind her and spoke slowly and quietly. 'Yes Miss Larkin that is fine. Take all the time you need.'

She thanked him. The full conversation she was dreading was over in less than twenty seconds. She was happy about this. She gathered a few personal belongings and her laptop, and Sadie came over to her.

'Shall I come over later?' she asked.

Meg thought about this and realised she just could not do with any more sympathy for one day. She quickly answered, feeling a little guilty, 'I am spending the night with my gran, but I will call you.'

Her friend's face seemed a little sad, but they then said their goodbyes. She vaguely remembered collecting the rest of her stuff and, as she did, a few staff members glanced at her with sympathy looks. Before he left his office, her boss appeared again and this time he looked like he had composed himself a little she thought, and this time he actually looked at her when he spoke. He offered his condolences and told her he fully understood her having time away and if there was anything the company could do for her, she should just ask. She began to feel as though she was having an out of body experience. She thought she had had this conversation earlier and it was done. She now felt as if he was the one telling her she was not going to return, basically telling her she was leaving and there was nothing could be done. It was as if it was not her standing there in that room, it was another person, and she was watching. She flinched and this brought her back to the present and she realised he was waiting for her to speak. After a few seconds she was able to feel the confident Meg reappearing.

'Oh it won't be a long time, maybe a few weeks,' she said reassuringly and again his face seemed to drop into a frown. 'I will just collect a few things then I will be off.' she added, heading for the door.

'Thank you, Miss Larkin, you have been an asset to this company since you started here,' he said. This statement took her aback a little. Again, it was as though she was leaving for good.

She quickly replied, 'Oh, you haven't seen the last of me yet.'

And with a smile she left. She just needed to get out of there. Outside, the sky was blue and the birds were singing. She walked a few blocks before starting to feel very dizzy and nauseous. She sat on the nearest bench she could. As she sat she looked down at the box. The entirety of her personal office belongings on her knee in her tote bag. She had never felt so alone. She tried to focus on a sparrow nearby and breathed deeply until the dizziness subsided. She was then able to walk the short distance to the comfort and serenity of her own home.

CHAPTER 3

OPPORTUNITY

When Meg arrived home, she tried to busy herself putting her office belongings safely away. She placed her laptop on her living room table and plugged the cord in the plug socket ready for when she felt able to log on – hopefully in a few days she anticipated. She went to her bedroom and found her box of personal stuff and gently lifted it down from its shelf and as she did the phone rang. It was her gran, again, reminding her to take her pills. They chatted for around five minutes and eventually Gran was getting a little distraught. Meg felt she could not cope with this so she told her she felt really well and that she should not worry herself for the time being. Meg ended the call by telling her gran she loved her and pretending someone was at the door.

She placed her personal box onto the bed, opening it, and as she did so a few of her precious photographs spilled out. She picked them off her bed covers and studied them. There was one of her parents, smiling lovingly at each other on their wedding day. It was a portrait, just of their heads, the background all white and hazy, clear looks of love and joy on both their faces. Another was a family one, she spotted her gran in a smart navy-blue suit, short brown curls framing her face, pink-rouged cheeks and pink lipstick, looking very dapper, Meg grinned to herself. It was nice to see her gran like this, as nowadays Meg was used to the little grey haired, chubby, older lady she saw in front of her on a daily basis. Meg took her gaze to her father in the photograph. He was in his army uniform, looking so handsome, her mother stood beside him, a lot smaller than his large frame, thus making her bend her head a quite a lot as she was gazing up into his eyes lovingly.

Meg picked up another photograph. It was her favourite, a photograph of her when she was around five years old. This was probably one of her most cherished photographs. Her mother was by her side, her arm around Meg, and Meg was smiling a toothy grin and her father was smiling down at his daughter tenderly. Such a beautiful and perfect scene. Meg smiled and felt a slight tear in one of her eyes. She pulled herself away from the photographs and placed them neatly back in the box. Her box, her memory box. She busied herself again, slowly sorting through her office stuff, placing a few documents into the top of the box and also tidying some of her private paperwork. As she did so, she absentmindedly left her passport on the top of the paperwork in the box before placing it back in its original place. She then wandered aimlessly around the house and found herself going into the kitchen where she immediately felt a sudden thirst. She opened the fridge: water? juice? wine? After the morning she had experienced she immediately knew what the choice was. She poured herself a large glass of wine, drinking it while going to the bathroom and subsequently running a bath.

She placed the half-full wine glass on the edge of the bath and immersed herself in the hot bubbles of the bath. She lay there, sipping her wine, enjoying soaking in the lovely warm water, her thoughts dreaming of faraway places. She almost fell asleep. She shook herself awake, then reluctantly got out into the cool air. She dried herself, put on a pair of her comfy pyjamas and wandered into the kitchen, searching for food this time, as a sudden ravenous feeling started to overwhelm her. She opened the fridge again and noticed there were a couple of prepacked meals, a half-eaten quiche and some left-over pizza but apart from those, not much else that looked appetising. She decided on the pizza taking in its delicious aroma as she reheated it. She plated it up and slowly poured herself another glass of wine and started to eat the food quite gluttonously. As she did so, she really relished the taste and was totally absorbed in this delight.

Distracted by the delicious food, she reached for more of the new painkillers to try and numb the pain that had been getting steadily worse all afternoon. Feeling full from her snack and feeling quite relaxed, she decided to go and have a lay down. As she lay on her bed her thoughts slipped back to the happy photos of her family. She smiled, remembering the happy memories of her childhood and the constant love and adoration from her parents. She lay there and thought of her gran, her dear gran, reminiscing about their adventures together, the holidays and the constant love and protection her gran had given to her. Her gaze then fell on the window. It was dusk now; she always loved this time of the evening, when everything seemed to be winding down, the sky gently losing its natural light, the hum of the traffic slowly dispersing and peace emerging at the end of the working day. She stared at the window and the dusk for a while, totally relaxed and feeling contentment, then gradually fell asleep.

She awoke quite alarmed and for a few seconds she had no idea where she was, and panic started to flow through her body. Eventually reality started to kick in and she realised she had napped, that was all. She gazed over at the bedside clock. It was 8.45pm and the room was dark, full of shadows. Her head felt very clear and for the first time in hours, her headache had totally gone. Must be the new tablets that I did not want, she considered, I must keep taking them then if it means feeling like this. She got up off the bed, and as she did so a rush of energy riveted through her body. In that moment she felt alive, really alive, a feeling she had not had in months. It was if there was new blood gushing though her body, pumping through every single vein, making her heart strong and in that moment, she felt she could accomplish anything. Wow what a feeling! She let herself relish this newfound feeling for a good few minutes, not wanting it to subside, before realising she was once again hungry. She rushed out of her bedroom, straight to the kitchen and made straight for the fridge. As she passed the front door she noticed a white envelope on the door mat. Must have missed that earlier, she thought, picking it up.

It was quite official looking, her name and address typed in full, but as she examined it closer she thought at the same time it was quite quirky with holiday emojis printed all around the outer edge. She opened it not knowing what to expect. Was it an invitation? If it was, that would be the last thing she wanted. She sliced the envelope open. Out fell an official-looking piece of paper with gold edging. The invitation was short and quite to the point. Her name was printed on the top and, reading further, it explained she had been selected for a free all-inclusive mini-cruise. She read further down the invitation, not knowing if this was for real. She was invited onboard the maiden voyage of a new: *'Traditional, luxurious and welcoming ship.'*

She read more: *'This is a new concept in holiday ships, a grand, personalised experience which awaits you on this cruise ship. Your mini-cruise will be tailored to your unique needs, and you will have full autonomy during your holiday'*.

She read it all again, looking for any typo errors showing it was a hoax, but she could not find any, and it did seem to read quite legitimate. What the heck she thought? She could not remember entering any competitions. Then she noticed the ticket which was on the floor at her feet and which must have fallen from the envelope in her haste to open it. The ticket was also gold-edged and she noticed in the top right-hand corner a little gold emblem of a ship. It truly was eye catching and unique. She read her name which was in full, even my middle name she contemplated. Below her name were her full address, phone number and email address. She was mystified.

She read further down the ticket, and this part seemed more like instructions than an actual ticket. This has got to be a scam, she thought to herself, but as she read further down but everything was on there right in front of her eyes. She decided to put it one side and think about it as she made a snack. As she sat eating her food, her thoughts went back to the ticket. If it was a scam, where was the phone number on it which would evidently charge her a fortune for ringing it? She picked it up and studied it once more. There was definitely no phone number and no email link either and no forwarding address. She looked closely and to her alarm she noticed the date for the cruise was the very next day. She re-read the instruction part of the ticket and it clearly stated a taxi to Port Leedham which was her local port, was included and that it would be waiting at her address the very next day at 9am. How convenient – if this was legitimate.

Leedham, the town Meg lived in, was situated near to the sea and that was one of the things she had always loved about living there. It had all the amenities of a small town and she never had to travel far for anything. It had a good assortment of shops. These included a supermarket, a couple of antique shops, a bakery, a small cinema, a few quaint coffee shops, and it had its own library in the very centre of the town square. Meg's house was in the middle but she could enjoy the sea breeze and the small beach and there was a small port which was situated at the far end of the town. She loved living there and could not think of living anywhere else, and it had the added advantage of her gran's house being conveniently just up the hill.

Meg weighed up the invitation of the mini-cruise and slowly decided that, if it was legitimate, then the taxi would be there the very next morning. She decided to take the opportunity, even if it was a scam; she felt like taking a chance for once. She needed something to take her mind off things and if she got to the designated place and it was a hoax then she could just go back home again. Taking a chance card, that was what she felt she was doing, and she started to feel a new sense of excitement.

She started to think about what she would pack and realised she had to do it that evening. She found herself opening her wardrobe and contemplating what she would take on her little break. She started to pull items from the rails and added clothes which included some sun wear, a party dress, a formal dress, a pair of high heels, lastly she put in her comfy jogging pants and trainers. Oh, and I may need a cardigan, she pondered as it was only April and it maybe cool on the ship in the evening. After packing the clothes in her suitcase she then scurried to the bathroom and emptied her cabinet. She tipped the contents into her ditty bag and then emptied the full contents of her make-up bag onto her dresser and chose the items she thought she would need for her trip. As she zipped up her make up bag, she felt a huge sense of exhilaration and enthusiasm for her forthcoming trip. She re-read the in invitation, and it confirmed that the cruise was all-inclusive. Just minimal stuff needed then, her mind wandering to the endless glasses of wine, the cocktails and nibbles, the relaxation – everything she needed to take her attention off the events of the last few months.

Within an hour she had packed her small suitcase full of clothes and the essential items she thought she might need. She retrieved her passport from her personal box, glad she had left it on the top. She was scurrying around with excitement, finding her phone charger and carefully making sure she had enough of the new wonder-drug tablets for the trip.

She tried to ring her gran to tell her the good news but there was no answer. Then she remembered: her gran had said she was at one of her meetings that night so she would not be able to answer. I will ring her tomorrow, Meg thought, when I am safely on that ship, and that way my gran will not be able to talk me out of it. She smiled to herself. Her gran was not the type to take chances and would never do anything as absurd as this. And anyway, Meg thought, her gran was always more preoccupied with the dead rather than the living and hearing the dead whisper and speaking with them. Meg started to feel the familiar infuriation at her gran's interest and her gran's borderline obsession with the afterlife. Anyway, she thought, the cruise is only a few days long. She hoped her gran would not even notice she had gone.

Meg texted Sadie but did not go into detail, just messaged her that she was taking a few days away and she would call her when she got back. She did not receive a reply but thought she might just be busy.

CHAPTER 4

NEW HORIZONS

The pick-up was right on time. The taxi driver examined her ticket before putting her luggage in the trunk, then he opened the back door for her. Chivalry still exists, she thought and thanked him and smiled to herself as she got in, relishing in the comfy leather seats. She managed to have good look at the driver. He was quite old, looked quite robotic in a weird sort of way and was wearing a smart black uniform and white shirt. She tried to make small talk, but he was focused on the road so after a few attempts, she gave up.

They reached their destination quite quickly. Megan felt a great surge of excitement as she saw the cruise ship anchored in the port, floating on the crystal-blue sea. So, it was real! she thought, feeling more and more excited. She had been selected, along with god knew how many others, for this luxury cruise. Maybe if she enjoyed it enough there might be a catch –that she would have to sign up for another cruise and pay the full cost next time. She was not bothered in the slightest; she needed the break.

As she got out Meg took a few minutes to gaze at the immense splendour of the ship. It was huge although it did look rather vintage. She noticed the immense chimney being the focal point of the outside of it, its wall rising up through the whole of the ship, its tip towering over the full expanse. She also noticed the mast. From her experience of cruises, she knew most modern-day cruise ships did not have them anymore so this must be an old cruise liner. She hoped it would be more modern inside. She could clearly see the taff rail around the higher open decks towards the back of the ship and noticed it was a brass colour – very unusual but exquisite. She started to follow the other passengers towards the gangway and as she did, she glanced at the side of the ship and noticed there were no balconies. The side of the ship seemed like a cliff of endless windows of outside cabins. Oh well, what did I expect for free? she thought, quite disappointed at the fact that she was not going to have a room with a balcony.

Meg made her way up the gangway and onto the ship and noticed other robotic like individuals, all dressed in black suits and white shirts delivering more luggage. It was almost mystifying, she thought, watching their machine-like actions. . She reached the reception area where a small queue was forming. On entering reception she was totally taken aback: the whole area was very glamourous – in stark contrast to the outside of the ship. There were two magnificent marble gold-coloured columns in the centre of the lobby, a highly polished marble floor spreading itself out into each corner of the area, and a she took the scene in she realised everything was in the same gold and cream colour scheme; it reminded her of the tickets. She loved the attention to detail. How exquisite, she thought. There were two massive staircases that entwined around the reception desk. Each of the steps appeared as if they were glass and illuminated, giving off a warm glow. There was delicate brass rose garlands which entwined their way down each of the handrails. The staircases meandered their way up to the next level which she could see was a mezzanine floor and again appeared to be totally made of glass. The mezzanine floor was probably the most imposing feature of all, and it was complemented by a massive gold-and-brass chandelier that was hanging precariously above the dead centre of reception. There were four lifts almost symmetrically placed around the staircases. They looked very elegant and were made completely of glass. There were also lots of gold-edged mirrors scattered on the walls, looking very imposing but at the same time making the area feel twice as big. Scattered around were shiny brass urns, and she noticed every door in the reception was cream and had brass handles to match. This scheme had been clearly thought-out, she reflected and thought to herself that it was almost over-the-top but also very classy looking and she liked it.

Eventually it was her turn in the queue. The receptionist smiled, selected a pass from the masses on the shelf behind her and passed her the little plastic card. The receptionist seemed unusually quiet as she gestured towards the lifts. Meg looked down at her pass. It was a small plastic cream card, delicately laced with a gold edging, a little gold ship in the top right-hand corner and her room number 311 etched on it. She realised at once it was the same design as the invitation and ticket. How beautiful, she reflected as she scrutinised it once again. Deck three then, room 11 it was, she reflected. She smiled and thanked the receptionist.

She entered one of the glass lifts , and as she did so she observed that the gold edges on the glass exactly matched the mirrors in reception. She pressed the gold button for deck three and found her cabin almost at once and gently swiped her pass in the door slot. Once inside she was pleasantly surprised. It was indeed an ocean view, as she had thought, with a very large square sea-view window. Gold blinds edged the window, and she immediately went over and opened them fully so she had a clear view of the ocean. The cabin seemed very spacious with a queen-size bed sprawling itself in the middle of the room. Complimentary chocolates were beautifully placed in a rose-shaped box on her bed. She looked around more and again noticed that the cabin had some of the classy gold-and-brass touches as the reception but also was quite minimalistic, just one painting on the wall, of a flower garden, and one large gold-edged mirror on the wall opposite the bed. She liked minimalistic; it made her feel more like she was at home.

She immediately felt settled in her new room for her journey. She opened the fridge and was happy to see there was a mini-bar inside, including wine, spirits and snacks. Very nice, she thought, opening the wine, pouring it gently into a gold-edged wine glass. Taking a cool mouthful of it she relaxed.

Ahh relaxation, just what she needed. She took her pills from her bag, swallowed them with a mouthful of the wine and then headed over to the bathroom and took a quick peek. It was small but immaculately clean, complimentary toiletries all stood on the shelf in a line. 'Lovely,' she whispered as she sipped more of the wine, totally happy and glad she had taken the chance card. She then noticed her luggage standing in the doorway; it had been delivered discreetly and she did not even know when!

CHAPTER 5

CUISINE

After showering and changing, she thought she would take a look around the ship. As it was getting on for lunchtime she decided to go and check out the restaurants. According to the ticket's instructions, they were situated on decks four, five and six. She took the glass stairs, slowly this time, still taking in the ship's scenery and feeling quite in awe of it all. She touched the delicate brass roses on the handrails and smiled. She felt happy.

She followed some individuals up the magnificent staircase and it was clear they too were making their way for something to eat. She glanced and smiled at two of them and was rewarded with a couple of smiles back. She had a wander and looked at each of the restaurants; there were two on that deck. There was the 'Steak Lounge', which looked as if it was American themed and informal, whereas the other was a formal but very pretty looking French restaurant named the 'Bateau Delectable Cuisine'. She knew that the name meant floating delectable cuisine from her French classes at school and a small smile etched its way from the corners of her mouth as she remembered the memories of her schooldays. She pondered the choices and decided to look around on the other decks before choosing where to have her lunch.

On the next deck she came across the main restaurant. This was a lot bigger than those she had already seen. It seemed to be more open-space dining. It was a marketplace, buffet style restaurant. She had been on a few ships that had this type of buffet restaurant. This restaurant was towards the front of the ship, long glass windows down each side letting in a lot of light, giving the restaurant a light and airy feel. This was definitely the informal restaurant of the ship. She could see, over at the front, there was an open-to-the-air dining section for the warmer days which the hazy spring sunlight was already trying its best to light it up even more than the inside. This looked a very appealing sight. She immediately knew this was where she would take her lunch. She loved the atmosphere already and was feeling quite relaxed.

She noticed the tables were a light cream colour, each with a cream tablecloth with a gold edging. This remined her of her ticket and room pass and she smiled at its familiarity and the attention to detail on the ship's behalf. She noticed the chairs were cream and matched the tables perfectly, with an upholstered seat for comfort and little gold studs on each. She looked up and there were three massive gold-and-glass chandeliers which gave off a warm and bright natural aurora, making the full room very bright and fresh-looking. As she wandered round, taking in counter after counter of food. Not only were there massive amounts of food on each of the counters, there was cuisine to suit everyone's taste and culture. She took her time, patiently deciding what she wanted to eat. There was no rush, she told herself even though her stomach was rumbling again. She picked some roast chicken and some pasta and chose a Greek salad to accompany it. Everything was self-service, not just the food, which was quite the normal in this type of restaurant, but even the drinks which was quite unusual for a cruise ship. She had been on a few cruises before, and she had always been able to choose and serve her food herself but then it had been waiter service for drinks. How unusual, she thought, this is what the ticket must have meant when it stated full autonomy – help yourself!

She placed her food on a table near the front deck. That way she could feel a slight sea breeze but it still felt very warm, the sunlight peering in, making it warm and pleasant. Perfect! she thought to herself. She went over to the bar. There was every drink you could think of on the bar, from water, juices, tea and coffee to wine, spirits and even, at the end of the bar, freshly made cocktails, lots of them, much to her delight! This was very strange, she thought, but she was just happy and chose a very large glass of wine to accompany her meal.

As she was enjoying her meal, she could not help but notice that the passengers were of all age groups of adults and there were no children and, unexpectedly, all the adults seemed to be on their own. She was quite surprised at the diverse adult age group on board, not that she felt it was just older people who went on cruises. She began to realise that there were no groups of passengers, no families; it was just people on their own, just like her. She began to wonder if this cruise invitation was for adults only and it had been intentional to invite single adults to help people make friends and socialise. Just as she was having these thoughts the ship's horn broke into them harshly, making her jump, informing everyone they were setting off. After realising this, a bolt of excitement ran through her body.

After eating her lunch, she was feeling a little thirstier so she went back over to the bar. She considered each cocktail before choosing a mojito. She wandered to the outside part of the restaurant and decided the April sun was warm enough to sit out in. She relaxed into a chair, enjoying the tang of the lime and savouring the mint flavour of the cocktail, placing her hand in her bag and taking her pills.

After her meal she decided to ring her gran. She knew that her gran could not stop her from going now she was out of port. She tried a few times but no reply. It was Wednesday though, she thought to herself, her gran's shopping day. She would call her later.

After lounging in the sun for at least another hour and one more cocktail later, she decided to go for a walk around. On the deck above she found two other restaurants. One was a Thai restaurant and the other was Italian themed. She took a peek in both and noticed, much to her dismay, that they were both self-service as well. Although she would prefer to pick her own food in the buffet, she still revelled in the idea of waiter service in a restaurant. It was the norm, she thought to herself – who has Italian cuisine buffet style? She quickly dismissed these thoughts as she felt the invigorating sway of the ship moving slowly towards the open ocean. She took a deep breath and breathed in the fresh smell of the sea.

While wandering she managed to find the full open deck on deck nine. It was quite breezy up there and she was glad she had put her cardigan on and huddled into it. As she approached the deck, she noticed the ship's big chimney, which was smoking, and she felt a gush of warm air in the atmosphere from it, which made her unexpectedly shudder. Nothing much up here, she thought to herself, again shuddering, so she decided to go back down the decks to a warmer place and hopefully find another bar. As she did so she thought about how, up until then, she had experienced the odd smile or nod from other passengers but she had, deep down, felt a little isolated. It was as though everyone else had their own priorities and were not concerned in making conversation with her. Now this would normally have been fine as she was content with her own company. But as the day went on she became more curious and started to crave a little human company.

She made her way downstairs and found the Mozart bar, one of the many bars on the ship. This was an authentic-looking bar from the 1970's, she mused. It was as though this bar had been left untouched. It had a deep maroon carpet throughout its expanse. Red velvet sofas and chairs, all matching, spread out around mahogany oval-shaped coffee tables. The actual bar was in the middle of the room and was a complete circle, its counter following the mahogany theme. It reminded her of an old working men's club and she laughed at this thought – maybe out loud as a passenger glanced at her and smiled. She noticed it was very busy in this bar and there were lots of passengers enjoying the free drinks and snacks. As she looked around further, she realised the bar was not attended – how strange. There was every drink you could think of on the bar and passengers were just helping themselves. Why not? she thought – the trip was all inclusive. She approached the busy swarm of passengers and reached for a strawberry daiquiri cocktail. As she did so her hand slipped on the glass, and she almost spilled it on the woman at the side of her. After apologising, the lady smiled at Meg and Meg smiled back at her. She asked if Meg would like to sit at a table with her. Meg took the opportunity for some human company and chose to sit with her. The women had a mass of curly blonde hair and wore blue eyeshadow and red lipstick. Meg could not help but feel the woman reminded her of a female pop star from the seventies and she chuckled to herself at these thoughts. She noticed the woman had a small portable oxygen tank with her and two small tubes were discreetly wrapped around her neck leading to her nose. They chatted for a while and Meg found out her name was Carol and that she fifty-one years old. Carol was not very well, cystic fibrosis as she explained to Meg, and it was not good either as she was in the latter stages. Carol pointed to her oxygen tank. Meg gave a look of sympathy towards the poor woman but was not ready to disclose anything about her own condition. She did not want to talk about it – she had come on this cruise to forget about it. So she carried on with some polite conversation but really, she pondered , to be honest illness was the last thing she wanted to hear or talk about. After a while she made her excuses and had another wander around and found the piano bar.

This room was in stark contrast to the cream-and-gold scheme of the rest of the ship she had seen so far. As she entered, she heard soothing music and was quite in awe of its grey, silver-and-white interior. Each wall was a gey/silver colour, and this, in contrast almost made the walls look as though they were glass. It was very modern, and Meg's focus moved to the middle of the room and rested on the grand piano. This was a modern piano, gloss white with delicate black edging which totally matched the piano keys. The piano had a glass bar which curled itself around the sides of it. She had never seen anything like this. There were silver, space-like stools placed in front of the bar part so a person could actually sit at the bar while the piano was being played – very ingenious. There were other tall silver bar tables scattered around the room with silver matching bar stools. White lights were nestled in between each table, their brilliant and dazzling light making the room feel bigger than it actually was. She noticed this room was not carpeted like the others she had seen. It had a shiny wooden floor, a grey gloss colour, buffed to perfection. It was then that Meg noticed that the main bar which was along the back wall. It shone vividly in the bright lights and it seemed to be made of pure glass. She could not help but walk towards it and, as she did so, she was able to inspect it more closely. It was indeed glass she thought, as she ran her hand along its surface and then she noticed it was rimmed by beautiful, delicate silver edging. The edging ran all the way around it and the same silver stools were placed in front of it. Again, there was every drink Meg could think of. She gently sat on one of the stools and selected a drink, this time a glass of pinot grigio. As she sat, she listened to the soothing Rhythm and Blues music which was coming from the speakers at the far side of the bar. The grand piano, although it was a splendid sight and the focus point of the room, sadly sat unoccupied. Strange, she thought, and then realised she was the only one there! The others will soon discover this, she pondered, and it will soon be full of people so I may as well make the most of the solitude. She was enjoying the peace and relaxation much too much to care.

As she was sat enjoying yet another glass of wine and revelling in the solitude, a few others did eventually enter the bar. She watched as most made their way to the unmanned bar, some were greedy taking two or three drinks and scurrying to their seats as though they had stolen something. Others were cautiously selecting one drink at a time, looking around as if someone was going to come out of the shadows and take it from them. She sighed and thought to herself – people!

It was in that second she felt a slight movement of the ship: the first time she had actually felt she was moving on her journey, reminding her she was at sea and on her way to the next port. She gazed around some more. She now started to take in more of the events of the past two days. She began to think about her gran and how upset she had looked at Meg's consultation. It was probably taking its toll on her gran more than on herself, Meg thought sadly. She wished she could take the whole thing away from both her gran's and her life. She wished she could just erase the last two months, and start again from where she was happy with no cares in the world. Well, she could while she was on this cruise, she thought happily. 'I am me, no illness, no inhibitions, just me here to enjoy myself,' she thought, a happy feeling overwhelming her. She recalled her earlier thoughts, and as she looked around once again, she noticed that each passenger was on their own. There did not seem to be families present, just individuals. How strange?

Just as she thought it might be time to make her way back to her cabin for a lie down. As she did so, she was jolted by a scream. She jumped up and noticed that a woman was on the floor gasping for breath. She moved closer to see what was happening.

The woman was clutching at her chest and making rasping noises. It seemed clear she needed help. Meg looked around for medics or anyone. The other passengers started to try and to help the poor woman and Meg also tried to help her. She glanced around, looking for a member for staff or a first aider, but there did not seem to be anyone around except the passengers. The vision before Meg's eyes was one of chaos. A passenger was trying to give CPR while another was running around frantically trying to get help. The situation escalated and eventually Meg realised the poor woman had lost her battle for life. Passengers were distraught, as was Meg. She moved away, not wanting to watch anymore and not being able to believe what she had just witnessed. As she was walking away, she noticed only what she could think she remembered as four individuals all dressed the same in a black uniform as the taxi driver, pushing a shiny steel trolley, its wheels making an irritating squealing sound on the deck floor. The woman's body was placed on it and quickly wheeled away by the four nonchalant individuals. Meg scurried back to her cabin, feeling nauseous at what she had just witnessed. Reaching for her pills, she decided she would stay there the rest of the day. Her thoughts kept wandering to the episode in the bar. She was not sure if it was the alcohol taking its toll or if she was remembering it correctly, but it was all so weird. Either way she had a sleepless night in her cabin.

CHAPTER 6

RECOLLECTION

The next morning, the evening before a blurred vision, Meg was up and showered ready to take in the rest of her cruise. She tried to put the previous evening's experience behind her. As she wandered out of her cabin it seemed to her that there was a solemn atmosphere on the ship that morning. She went to the reception desk and patiently waited for the receptionist. She was going to ask about the previous day and to actually make sure what she had seen was not a dream. She must have waited a good five minutes, but no-one appeared. A little irate, she decided to go up to the main restaurant. She chose to sit out in the early morning sun on the breakfast deck, which was unusually quiet. She felt she needed a bit of peace so she could reflect. She grabbed a coffee, but her appetite had wavered. She picked at a few bits of fruit. Now she was sober, she tried to think of the events the previous evening. She tried to make sense of it but could not.

As she was eating a young man walked nearby, maybe in his middle thirties, she thought to herself as she took in his distinguished mop of red hair and beard to match. He was quite tall and she noticed his brass watch which looked almost too big for his thin wrist. She averted her eyes from this as he got nearer and then he gestured towards the seat opposite her. She smiled and waved her hand as he sat across from her at the table.

'Hi, my name's Steve,' he said politely. 'I hope you don't mind me sitting here.'

'No, it is fine,' she answered shyly. 'I am Meg. Pleased to meet you.'

He went on, 'I was just hoping someone would talk. It seems like everyone on the ship is pre-occupied and does not seem to want to chat.'

She smiled and replied .'Yes, I have been thinking that too. It all feels a little weird don't you think?'

He nodded. 'I cannot seem to grasp it but there is something not right. Ever since I opened that invitation I have thought something was amiss.'

Meg replied, 'Yes, me too – and isn't it weird that everyone seems to be on their own?'

He nodded. 'Yes, I think I am starting to regret taking up this cruise opportunity.' The look on his face was one of dread. 'And did you witness the unfortunate events of yesterday?'

She replied quietly, 'Oh dear, yes I did!' She felt a great sadness gushing through her. 'I did not know if it was a dream or I had actually witnessed that tragic event.'

'Oh, it was real all right,' he said with a grimace and she noticed a look of anger cross his face. 'Where were the staff? It seemed like nobody from the crew were there.'

She nodded and replied. 'Yes I agree. Did they really take her away on a trolley?'

He nodded again. 'Yes, they did. I saw it with my own eyes. I was really traumatised. I feel like I need to get off at the next port. That is another strange thing – we have not stopped at a port yet and no complementary information from the captain. Strange don't you think?'

The thought then hit her: they had not had any messages about the ports, the weather or even the pre-recorded safety stuff, how strange. Usually, the cruises she had been on, there was one day at sea but then every day a different port, a different adventure and intermittent messages from the captains. It started to dawn on her that she might be captured on this ship; she might be a prisoner. She dispersed the thought as quickly as it came but she nodded in agreement with his statement.

He carried on. 'Do you mind me asking, are you ill?'

His words rang a bell in her head. She took a few minutes to answer.

'Sorry, I didn't mean to intrude' he said. 'It's just that I am ill – I have pancreatic cancer, terminal. I thought this would be a good trip to go on and forget about it for a while.'

She grimaced, fear taking hold of her body once again, the familiar feeling of nausea creeping over her body.

He carried on,' Yesterday I managed to speak to another young man, and he had a terminal illness too, that has to be a link between us all.'

Meg thought about Carol from yesterday – she too had had a terminal illness. Meg felt a wave of panic rise and tried to steady herself. The man sitting in front of her was probably right in some way. Maybe everyone on the cruise had received an invitation to have a last holiday? She felt so confused.

After eventually composing herself, she was able to whisper to the man sitting across from her, 'Yes I do,' tears welling up in her eyes.

He studied her for a moment and said, 'I am so sorry. I did not mean to upset you.'

He handed her a napkin and she wiped her eyes and answered, 'It is okay, thank you but I don't want to talk about it really.' She composed herself a little. 'But I will try and find out more and if I do, you will be the first person I find and tell.'

He smiled and replied, 'I will do that too, thank you for speaking to me.'

She thanked him and, as he left, her mind was whirring around and around. She was trying to make sense of the matter. She hoped deep down this was just a holiday and it probably was some passenger's final one and that it would all be okay. But then she had another feeling. A feeling of utter dread of what may lay in store.

CHAPTER 7

RELAXATION

After eating her breakfast, Meg went up onto the open deck. She looked at the horizon. Sea, sea, sea, nothing else for miles. No dots on the horizon. Just the blue sky and deep blue sea. She grabbed a glass of wine from the pool bar, choosing what she wanted as there was no bar attenders. She walked over to one of the sun loungers, which were neatly arranged around the pool – very methodically, she caught herself thinking. She slightly moved one just because she could. And feeling a little like a rebel she slipped off her shoes, laid back on the lounger and placed the tip of her sunhat over her eyes. She fumbled in her bag, not getting up until she found the bottle of pills. She swallowed them with a sip of the wine and relaxed, probably for the first time since she had boarded the ship. She felt the sun's rays beating down. It was a weak April sun but nonetheless was created a lovely warming feeling through her body. She felt content for a while and just laid there enjoying the spring warmth. She was aware of a few others starting to occupy the other loungers but did not avert her gaze from under her hat.

She wanted to be alone. She wanted an hour of solace and peace. She must have fallen asleep as she woke with a start. She flinched as she felt a cold chill on her legs. She sat up and realised the sun had gone, hidden by a few grey menacing clouds. The others had dispersed too, she looked at her phone. It was 4.15pm. Where had the time gone? she thought, must have been asleep ages. She looked at the empty glass of wine beside her. Yes, she wanted another, she thought as she gathered up her bag and shoes. She chose a merlot wine this time and wandered into the inside bar. This bar had afternoon sandwiches, nibbles and desserts set out at the furthest end. Her eyes gazed over to the mini-cake section. Just the one, she thought smiling to herself as she took it and sat in the corner by the window. There was no one else in the bar, but it was getting later, she thought – they must be showering, getting ready for the evening. She was enjoying herself way too much eating the cake and drinking the wine to want to go anywhere just yet.

She gazed through the ship's window at the ocean. It was so memorising, slow ebbing waves lashing at the sides of the ship almost like a cat licking its milk. A calming sight, she had not felt this calm in months. She reached in her bag for more painkillers but stopped. She had no headache, and this was a strange feeling as she had learned to live with the constant headaches. She realised that it was an emerging habit to just to keep popping the pills. A thought flickered in her mind: should she take them anyway just to make sure? She toyed with the idea until her subconscious decided for her, yes just take them. She reasoned with herself as she swallowed them with more wine: that the headaches had gone because she had taken them so regularly.

After a while of staring at the ocean she decided to get up. As she stood up she felt a surge of energy through her entire being. She smiled. She liked this new body she had. She had not felt as well as this in months. Her aches and pains had disappeared as quickly as the sun earlier. She felt a warm glow running through her veins, it was as though there was constant adrenaline being pumped into her veins. She almost felt like skipping and she decided to go and have a shower before the evening.

CHAPTER 8

NEW IMAGE

As Meg showered, she revelled in the peace and tranquillity of the warm water and the stillness of her mind. She found herself humming to herself and felt happy. Happiness had been short in supply the past few months, so she relished the moment. She decided she would eat at the French restaurant that evening and looked forward to dressing up for a change. She eventually got out of the shower, dried herself and shook her long dark hair, smiling at the natural curls and waves that emerged from it. She glanced in the mirror at her reflection. Gone was the drawn face, the sad eyes, the yellowed skin, the sad lips. Smiling back at her was a young woman, looking fruitful and positively glowing. Her skin was a healthy pink, her eyes sparkled and there was a definite twinkle there. She dressed in a long red dress. It was one of her favourites. She put a black shawl round her shoulders and selected black heels. She put on minimal make-up, finishing it off with a rouge lipstick. She clipped a small heart-shaped gold necklace to her neck – a present form her gran – and as she did so, she remembered she had not phoned her gran again. She must do it when she was ready – she must not forget. Although, she thought, Gran was usually on the phone two and three times a day to her, and she found this a little strange. Putting that thought away for later, she studied her reflection in the long mirror. The dress snuggled every curve of her body, and her height really showed off the long dress length, finishing off with a provocative split to the side. She knew she looked good, and she felt a surge of commendation for herself. After months of feeling drab, depressed and forgotten, here was this woman standing in front of her, a vision who looked every bit as beautiful as the day she had turned eighteen. With this new-found confidence she grabbed her red clutch bag and left for the restaurant.

There were already some passengers in the Bateau Delectable Cuisine Restaurant when she arrived. She noticed a few admiring glances her way from both the male and female audience. She blushed a little but was also very thankful for the praising looks as they gave her a little buzz of excitement. In the corner there was a little stage with a harp placed in the middle. She noticed there was no one playing it, which would have been nice, she thought. Instead there was calming music coming from delicately hidden speakers.

Towards the other end of the restaurant she noticed delicately laced bronze-effect shutters. She could not figure out if they were real lace or polyester but even so they looked gorgeous. She wondered what was behind them. She took a seat at a solo table. She was then aware of the shutters opening. They revealed food, masses of it, all French cuisine. Oh no, not buffet again! she thought, why can't I just be waited on, for just once. Other passengers were staring at the shutters too, some giving looks of disgust and despair. A few wandered over and Meg did too, after a while. The food did look very appetising and seemed very authentic and unique to France. There were the famous frogs' legs, mussels, some molasses that Meg was not sure of, and almost every other French dish you could think of. She started to pick out the most appetising items from the starter section and place them delicately on her plate, then choosing her main, which was a Bouillabaisse, and adding this to her tray as well. She went over to the bar and chose a cocktail. This time she opted for Margarita, choosing the one with the biggest piece of lime on it. She took everything carefully over to her table and began to revel in the fresh taste of the shellfish and the crusty French bread. As she sat there enjoying the peace and tranquillity and really enjoying the exquisite food, she felt a sense of fulfilment and contentment. When she had cleared her plate she contemplated a second helping. She walked over and chose a peach and goat's cheese tartine which looked wonderful! She also picked up another large glass of wine to accompany it.

She deliberated to herself as she ate another course that she had not enjoyed food like this in a long time. Each mouthful was magnificent. She was in food heaven and loved every minute of it. She remembered she had to take her pills and got them from her bag and washed them down with the alcohol. As she did so she watched the other guests. She noticed most of them were helping themselves to more courses. She even noticed one young man who had his plate stacked with food and she was sure he went over three or four times. What the heck she thought, let him enjoy himself! Dessert was even more exquisite. Lots of French fancies and desserts including a *creme brulé* which she could not resist. Feeling full and almost bursting, she decided she would go for a wander.

She wandered back along the deck towards the stern of the ship. It was windy and the ship was moving quite a lot now and she wished she had not worn the heels. She stared at the waves, which were getting bigger with each ebb, making a thunderous noise as they battered the ship's side. This was in very stark contrast to earlier in the afternoon. As she gazed ,it definitely did look quite stormy out on the deck now, and as the wind grew in strength so did the waves. The ship was rocking, and she had to cling onto the taff rail a few times and, as she did, she noticed it was actually wood. She had thought it was brass but it was just the goldish colour it had been stained. From past experience she remembered that old ships used wood for taff rails and the newer ships she had sailed on had steel rails, so this is a very old ship really. She darted straight for the next set of double doors which were at the most back-part of the ship. Once inside she realised, she was in some sort of music hall. She stood for a few seconds catching her breath from the wind. She was then able to see she had entered through the doors at the side of the hall. She walked towards the centre and her eyes took in an amazing sight. In the centre was a huge brass stage. Its floor sparkled and seemed to be made of either glass or Perspex, tiny sparkles on it glistened in the lights beautifully. She stood for another few seconds and admired its unique beauty. There were two microphone stands at the very front, placed symmetrically. To the side were two oak-and-brass guitars leaning precariously on their brass stands. The brass drum-set took centre stage, shining magnificently in the lights and, lastly, at each end of the stage were two very beautiful-looking oak-and-brass violins. She moved closer to inspect all of these beautiful instruments further. She really was in awe of how elegant they were. She stood at the very front of the stage and gasped at their well-crafted, elegant appearance. As she did this, she also noticed two speakers, discreetly hidden behind the dark green velvet curtains right at the back of the stage. It occurred to her that these instruments were probably never played and were just there for show, and she began to feel a little deception in the air. Slowly she turned around and looked at the audience seats and realised there was no one in the room but her. How strange, she pondered.

The velvet green of the stage curtains was echoed by a dark green patterned carpet flowing throughout the room. Each chair was of oak and the padded seats were dark green velvet with little brass studs arranged down each one. There were two chairs placed diagonally to each table. This was continued throughout the room. The tables were round and made of a shiny oak. Each had a small lamp on, which had little shade that was dark green. The dark green colours and the oak made this part of the room feel very dark and almost menacing even though it had its own unique beauty in the design. A lot of thought and design had gone into this music room, she thought appreciatively, and it was a pity there was nobody else in it to enjoy its splendour. She decided to investigate further and walked up the brass railed staircase which took her up the mezzanine-floor part of the room. She was aware of the ship swaying and grasped the handrail for a few seconds to steady herself. As she stood there at the very top, she started to reflect that there was actually a better view from up there. She was able to see the sparkling stage and all its contents and somehow it seemed to be better lit and more joyful in atmosphere. But, looking around, she was alone, no other being was present.

She decided to wander back towards the front of the ship. She was just walking past the Bateau Delectable Cuisine Restaurant when she heard what she thought was someone choking. The sound of choking was getting louder and louder. She could hear people shouting for help. Her mind went into overdrive and she felt dread. She stopped dead in her tracks, a feeling of dismay rushing over her. She did not want to go around the corner but felt compelled to see what was happening and try and give help if she could.

She gathered her thoughts together and peered around the doorway. The image what struck her again was nonsensical. There was a gentleman who was grasping his throat and seemed to be choking. He was on the floor and there were a few passengers standing there helplessly around him, it was obvious they had no idea what to do. Meg was glued to the spot for a few moments, fear taking over her body just as it had at her last consultation. Then a few moments later her body seemed to go into overdrive, and she felt herself running over to the poor man and trying to stop him from choking and she heard someone screaming for help and realised it was her own voice. No help came. She frantically tried and tried to stop the poor man from choking, realising with horror he was slipping away. Eventually his body went limp, his face went a bluish colour, and the passengers were still stood there, shocked, just staring, rooted to the spot. She could do nothing more and could only watch as the life slipped away from the man's body. She wept as she held his lifeless body in her arms.

After a few moments she realised she could hear a familiar sound. Once again it was the shiny trolleys wheels making their whirring noise as they moved along the deck boards. She looked up and noticed the same staff members from the previous evening. Almost mechanically, they placed the man's body on the trolley before wheeling it away. They showed no emotion and did not utter any words, their eyes focused on their task. Within seconds the poor man's body was gone.

Meg felt utterly devastated. The room was spinning but she managed to find a chair. The other passengers who were present slowly dispersed, forlorn looks on their faces. Meg uttered some words to one of them, but he just put his head down in dismay and wandered off. Meg thought the only place she could find solace was her cabin. She bumbled her way to it and threw herself on the small bunk, crying hysterically. She must have dozed off but was awakened by what she thought sounded like cries for help. She couldn't be sure if she had dreamt it or it was real but either way she was starting to feel really concerned and the dread started to fill her whole body once again.

The noise was coming from just outside her cabin door. She listened intently just to make sure it was actually cries for help and not her imagination. Yes, she definitely could hear a woman's voice shouting and it was getting louder. She jumped up from her bed and opened her door. There was a crowd at the end of the corridor, just at the tip of the stairs. She quickly grabbed her door pass and went to see what was happening. People were huddled around the screaming woman, forlorn looks on their faces. She moved closer to see what they were standing around. The next scene filled her with utter terror. She could see a female laying on the deck, at the very bottom of the stairs. And as Meg got closer, she could see a mass of blonde hair. Her mind was in complete disarray. She recognised with horror it was Carol, the woman she had been speaking to the day before. Meg's body went numb. She gasped as the screaming stopped abruptly. She realised the Carol's body was now totally lifeless. There was a woman bent down beside Carol's body, who was weeping uncontrollably. Meg lowered herself to try and comfort the distraught woman. As she did so she heard an all too familiar sound. It was the wheels of the trolley making its way along the deck, the trolley – the *death* trolley, she thought. Again, there were four nonchalant individuals, and they picked up Carol's body.

Meg suddenly had a surge of energy and stood up to confront one of them. They were not going to get away with it again, she though angrily. She moved through the others until she was dead straight in front of one of them. She looked at him, her eyes piercing his face, but he looked away and did not give her eye contact.

'What is wrong with the crew?' she almost screeched at him.

He looked quite startled and again bowed his head.

'Are there no trained first aiders on this crew? For goodness' sake this is the third accident I have witnessed. Where is your supervisor?' Meg demanded.

His face was expressionless. He started to push the trolley along with the other three individuals, away from Meg and away from the crowd. She thought she had heard others mumbling insults too but was too furious to understand what their remarks were.

She found herself shouting, 'I will find out what is happening.'

She was aware the individuals hastily made for the exit with the trolley. She was mortified and steadied herself and someone said a few words to her but she could not take them in. She managed to sit herself on the bottom stair. Someone bought a shawl from out of nowhere and put it around her shoulders. Then the crowd slowly dispersed with looks of fear and sadness on their faces.

Meg sat there for a while, totally on her own, a heavy silence looming over the staircase. As she brought herself back to reality an awful thought struck her: would she be next? Would the next accident be her? Would it be her lifeless body laid on the trolley? These thoughts whirred around her mind. She reminded herself she had fought one illness and was not ready to die. She then thought: if it was a conspiracy, then her shouting at the crew could mean only one thing – they would take their revenge.

Well no they won't! She suddenly regained her confidence and composed herself. I am not going to be next, she thought to herself, no way, I am alive, and I am going to stay that way. She knew that what she had to do – she needed to go and investigate this cruise ship further and she knew exactly the door she needed to go towards.

CHAPTER 9

HORROR

Meg followed the tracks of the trolley and its occupant towards the door at the end of the corridor, but it was locked and needed some kind of pass to get through it. She thought about this for a minute before remembering she had seen some passes behind the desk on reception the day before as she waited for the receptionist. She hurried back to her cabin.

'I could go to reception and ask if divert the receptionist's attention or I could just go up there and hope, like the day before that, there's no one manning the desk, nip behind and take a few passes,' she thought to herself but actually whispering the words out loud..

As these e ideas were running through her head all at once, causing her bamboozlement, another idea came to her: she could ring her gran and explain everything that was happening and get her to send some kind of help. She reached for her phone. She noticed she had no missed calls which was very strange as her gran called her twice a day sometimes. She dialled Gran's number but the message on her phone kept repeating 'Incorrect number dialled'.

'What on earths the matter with this damn phone?' her feelings being said out loud, once again.

She tried twice more and got the same message. It was then she decided she would have to take matters into her own hands. She rifled in her case and got out on a pair of jogging pants and a t-shirt and hastily put these on, grabbed her cardigan and squeezed her feet into her old faithful comfy trainers. She needed to be dressed casually, she deliberated in case she had to make any hasty escape. She grabbed her phone and put it on silent – just in case – grabbed her room-pass, putting it in her jogging pants pocket and made her way upstairs to the reception lounge.

To her delight, as before there was no one on the desk. She waited around five minutes but no one appeared. She moved slightly so she was at the side of the desk and could see the staircase clearly. No one was on the stairs either, so she grasped the moment. She quickly slid behind the desk and grabbed a handful of the cream plastic passes, stuffing them into her jogging pants pocket, vaguely aware of putting them in the left pocket so she did not get them mixed up with her own room pass which she had placed in her right pocket earlier. She hoped and prayed that just one of them would open the door downstairs. She checked there was no one else around before she descended the stairs, down towards the lower decks.

She finally got to the door where she tried at least five passes, tried slotting them in both ways but the door would not open. Noises then appeared from the corridor and she heard someone or something moving from the other side of the door. She knew she had to hide. She quickly ran and stood behind a pillar at the side of the stairs. She was breathing sharply and tried to close her mouth, so it made no sound. She waited and realised it was two of the automaton trolley pushers coming through the door. She waited with gasped breath until they were out of sight before running back to the door, once again trying each pass hastily.

To her surprise, on about the eighth try, the door opened. She gasped with excitement or fright – she was not sure which – and carefully placed that pass in her other pocket so she didn't get it mixed with the others. Through the door lay another long corridor. At the end was what looked like a service lift. This lift was not glass like all the other lifts she had seen on the ship. It was oblong, and not a box shape like the others, and its doors were an obscured black colour and non transparent. There were also stairs at the side of it, no gold edged roses on this staircase. It was a dark, morbid grey-coloured, very dimly lit, metal banisters and steel pillars at the top.

She heard a bleep from the lift and looked for somewhere to hide. The steel pillar was the only place. She tiptoed over to it and huddled her body behind the cold metal column. Then she heard the lift open and heard someone coming along the corridor. With dread, she realised it was yet another trolley being pushed towards the lift. As it was pushed closer to the lift she quickly glanced through the banister and to her dismay there was what seemed like linen or something else, she wasn't quite sure.. As it passed her she thought it might be a person beneath the linen and this notion filled her with dread, but she could not see much and couldn't be sure. It was pushed into the service lift and as it opened, she could see it was just the width to fit a trolley with its minders.

She knew she needed to get out of there before she was seen and there was nowhere for her to go but back up towards the door as she had no idea what was below. She was going to do this but suddenly stopped in her tracks; She knew in that moment she could not run away from this situation – she needed to find out what was happening, if not just for her sake but the sake of all the poor passengers. If she went back up to the safety of her cabin there was no way she would be able to risk going back down there again ever, she deliberated and as she did so a feeling of anger overwhelmed her. She must help all the others; she couldn't leave them all on this forsaken ship! She knew she had to go down either by the lift or stairs and very soon, before they found out the passes had been stolen. She had to find out exactly what was going on. With a feeling of courage suddenly washing over her she decided there and then she would go.

She tiptoed down each stair, trying her best to be as quiet as she could. This was deck two she realised, as it was one deck below her cabin which was on deck three. As she got to the bottom of the stairs there was another door. Oh, I hope this one does not need a pass as well, she thought, feeling panic rise in her body. She went over to it and peered through the plain glass.

Her eyes did not seem to connect with her brain properly as she stared through the glass of the door. This was a sight she did not want to see. She gasped, out loud and then realised she had to be quiet, be silent for her own safety. Her gaze took in a massive, very wide room. It was very brightly lit and all white, almost clinical. It had no windows. It remined her of an operating theatre. Nearest the door and in plain view was a row of the familiar shiny trolleys, all placed symmetrically at the side of each other. She could see what looked like linen or blankets on a few of the trolleys. She moved nearer to the glass so she could get a better view. What she saw next held her rooted to the spot. It was not linen or blankets – it was people. People who were still and grey, lifeless, the thin white sheets barely covering their bodies.

She held in a stifled shriek and felt her legs give way, causing her to hit the floor. She sat there for a few seconds or minutes, she wasn't sure. Her mind was whirring; she had no idea. A feeling came over her and she knew she had to move, to keep moving so she was not seen. 'Escape' was the word that came to her mind. As she fumbled her way up, her body feeling heavy and her legs almost like jelly, her gaze turned to the glass as if by automation.

She then noticed something very familiar on one of the trolleys. A hand was extruding out over the side of one of them, from under the white sheet. A shiny brass watch was on its thin wrist. Meg knew then this was the man she had met the night before. She felt dread consuming her body as she moved nearer and noticed the mop of red hair showing through the stark white sheet. She gasped and knew she could not bring herself to look at this awful scene anymore.

Her gaze moving away from the trolleys, she could see the middle part of the room. She could not believe what was there, in front of her own eyes. In those few seconds Meg was consumed with horror. Along the full middle wall of the room were what could only be described as ovens. They reminded her of the refrigeration units in a morgue as she had seen on films, but these were definitely ovens with big brass-like round doors on them. It was hard for her to comprehend the sight in front of her.

She watched as two of the trolleys were pushed up to two of the ovens by a pair of black uniformed staff. The doors were opened and, as they were, a red aura filled that part of the room. She was sure she could feel the warmth and heat on the glass and instinctively backed away a little, gasping with dread. She could not believe what she saw next and stood rooted to the spot in complete terror. The two black-clothed individuals slid whatever or whoever were on the trolleys into the oven and banged the door shut, solid. Glued to the spot she watched as other trolleys were pushed up to each oven and the process was repeated, the bodies on the trolleys were each pushed into an oven, and finally, the last one, her companion. The door slammed tightly shut with a large bang.

A feeling of total horror and dread engulfed her body and as she tried to process these feelings, a devastating thought started to occur in her mind. These were incinerators, human incinerators, and she then realised with a shudder that that was where the smoke from the chimneys was coming from. Upon realisation of this, she felt dizzy, and she was aware of her legs, once again, giving way under her weight. Again, she fell to the floor, gasping for air. She looked up at the ceiling and tried her best to focus her eyes on a point to stop the room from spinning. She tried to breathe slowly and restrain herself from crying out and knew she had to be quiet. She eventually pulled herself together and regained a little composure. What the hell was going on? She knew she had to stay hidden and wait until whatever activity was happening stopped. It seemed like eternity but eventually the room became silent, and she got up from her hiding place. Through the glass she could see all of the trolleys were neatly lined up again at the end of the room empty, and each one of the ovens was locked shut, the staff had all dispersed and it was now deathly quiet.

She considered what to do next. She knew she dare not stay there any longer or take another look at the ovens. An overwhelming urge to escape came over her, to escape as fast as she could. She made for the staircase and ran up the stairs two at a time, trying her best to be quiet. As she did so reality really started to kick in. She realised that every passenger on this ship was at risk, at risk of dying and of being pushed in the oven like a piece of meat. What a horrific ending to a life, she agonised – this cruise was a clever hoax to kidnap and kill people. It was then the final thought dawned on her – she was not on a luxury cruise; she was, in fact on board some kind of death ship.

CHAPTER 10

ESCAPE

She made her way quickly up flight after flight of stairs, up deck after deck of the ship, trying to get as far away from the bottom deck as she could. She also noticed that there was a weird atmosphere – there did not seem to be anyone around. This was a godsend. As she climbed higher and higher up the decks, her mind was racing: where could she go? where could she hide? did she need to tell anyone? These thoughts engulfed her as she kept on ascending stair after stair, going further and further up each level of the ship.

She remembered deck nine from her previous wander and how that was pretty high up and, trying her best to be undiscernible , made her way up there. The rumbling noise was getting louder, and she was sure she felt the ship rocking although she wasn't sure if it was herself shaking with fear after what she had just witnessed.

When she reached the very top deck, she spotted a ladder which ran up the side of the ship's chimney. She glanced towards the edge of the ship. The waves were getting bigger and were crashing against the ship. It seemed like a full-scale storm out there. Should she jump? She was not the strongest of swimmers and thoughts of her body being tangled up with the ship's propellers washed over her. It was also getting dark. What should she do? She looked again at the chimney then ran towards the ladder and started climbing it, not sure if she would be seen but hoping there would be a good hiding place until she could figure out what to do about this unbelievable situation.

She squashed her body between the ladder and chimney and, as she did so, she felt its warmth and shuddered as she realised where this warmth was coming from. She reached for her phone, hastily looked at it and tried her gran's number but, to her dismay, there was no signal. Damn, she thought, and then was aware of the rumbling noise which was getting louder by the second and now she definitely could feel the whole ship swaying. She hung on to the ladder for dear life. Then she turned and saw what she thought was a massive wave on the horizon, coming straight towards the ship. She closed her eyes as this tsunami wave enveloped the ship.

CHAPTER 11

TRUTH

She awoke, not sure of where she was. Her eyes glanced around trying to take in her surroundings. It was still dark but eventually her eyes were able to focus, and she was able to the all-too-familiar outline of port in the distance. A familiar sight and, to her delight, it was Port Leedham the one she had set off from a few days before. She lay there a few more minutes and memories of the past few days came flooding back to her: the diagnosis, the holiday, the ship, the bodies, the wave. Feeling cold and damp she looked down at herself. Her t-shirt was wringing wet, her jogging pants were wet too, dirty grey marks down each leg. She noticed the left leg of her jogging pants was torn. She was wearing one trainer, but the other was missing. She felt for her phone. It was not anywhere on her body and she had no idea where it was.

She managed to stand, feeling a little dizzy, as she tried to work out what direction the town was. As she did so, she noticed something on the sand. She moved closer and realised it was her trainer. She picked it up from the sand, emptied its contents of sea-water and sand mixed together and, although it felt quite awful, she placed it on her freezing cold foot. Anything was better that having to walk around with nothing on her feet, she thought.

She stood and got her bearings and realised she had to get to the port first, then she would have an idea which direction to walk in. She started walking towards the port silently, wishing there would be someone there to help her. The port drew closer and she now wished she had not put the trainer on at all. It was making squishy noises and she could feel the sharp grains of sand slowly chafing her foot.

As she approached Port Leedham, there seemed to be a small light coming from one of the buildings. She was amazed because the port did seem unbelievably intact considering she had just witnessed a tsunami. As she got closer, she headed for the building with the light but, as she did so, a feeling of disappointment washed over her when she realised it was only an outside security light. There was no one there; it was desolate. She turned and saw the lights of the town – her town, her home. She had to get to it. There was no help at the port. She hurried along in the direction of the familiar lights, her feet squelching in her trainers .

She walked until the port was just a dot on the horizon behind her. She was now near the main town square. She noticed her bedraggled reflection in the window of the library and sighed. She knew she needed to get home and fast. She could not bear anyone seeing her in this state. She tried to run but her body would not let her. Her legs felt jellified, so she slowed down to a fast walk. The image of her warm little house kept her going. Soon she was almost at the end of the terraces that were next to her street. She tried to quicken her pace but her body just would not allow her. As she reached the corner of her street, dawn was just breaking. She was vaguely aware of birdsong but was much too focused on her task to enjoy it.

She was there! She had made it to the safety of her house! She glanced at the amazing image of her little house and a feeling of hope ran thorough her body. She could not wait to get into its safety and warmth. She stood outside her door and a thought popped into her head: what about her keys? A few moments after, she remembered and reached under the pot on the top step and, sure enough ,the spare keys were there. What a godsend, she thought.

She entered her home. She felt the light switch and flicked it on. Walking into her kitchen an awful sight engulfed her – emptiness. Her legs started to buckle beneath her. She fell to the ground exhausted and shocked to her core. Empty? What had happened? She looked around once again – her kitchen was bare. Am I dreaming? she thought. She tried to focus once again and realised the sight in front of her was sadly real. She could not grasp what was happening. How? Why? She suddenly got up, finding a new release of energy, the adrenalin kicking in, pulsing through her veins. She knew she had to find out what was going on. She raced from empty room to empty room – the lounge, the bathroom, the bedroom.

'Where is all my furniture?' she gasped out loud. 'Where are my belongings?'

She was in total despair. She felt as if she was a spinning top, feeling dizzy and nauseous at the same time, with no idea what was happening to her. She found herself running around and around trying to make sense of it all. She even found herself outside, looking for anything of hers, inspecting the garden, bins, the shed. She could find nothing of hers, nothing at all.

It was like she did not exist anymore.

Then something triggered in her brain. Everyone must think she was no longer there. She was drowned by the tsunami wave, that was it! But she had only been gone three days? And as this thought sank in, she sat on the bare floor in her living room and reviewed this idea. She thought about what she could do next. She must have sat there at least twenty minutes or more. She sat and thoughts were running through her head at a fast pace. She tried to calm them and tried to think straight. She stared at her window and noticed it was now daybreak and, as she looked at this, she suddenly realised what she needed to do. She felt a sense of calmness and decided on her next plan of action: she must tell everyone she was alive, and she was safe and well. She could not take any more of this stupor . She needed to tell everyone the truth.

She fled from her house; she was going to sort this misunderstanding as fast as she could. She raced through the small streets, past the gates of the familiar park where she had spent many a happy childhood day, past the infant school where she had first learnt to write and past the small cemetery on her left.

She was now going up the hill, energy still racing through her being, towards her gran's familiar, cosy house. A feeling of warmth started to run through her cold, wet body, a feeling of familiarity and total love for her gran. She could not wait to see her again and feel her love.

There was a light on in the lounge as she made it to her gran's . She walked up the familiar path, up to her gran's front door. She tapped gently on the door, walked into the lounge and whispered:

'Gran, it's me.'

Her gran was by the fireplace and she turned to face Meg. A look of bewilderment came across her face and Meg picked up on this and wondered why? The look then turned to pure and utter love as her gran looked at her affectionally. Her gran started to speak softly, her voice full of emotion.

'My dear, I knew you would come and visit me.'

Meg replied, 'What do you mean gran? I have only been away three days! I did try calling you. My house....' She trailed off seeing the look on her grans face.

Anna's gran was now frowning a little and her lips were trembling as she began to speak. 'I am sorry, Meg, but you cannot be here, you need to be at rest.'

Meg felt as though the blood was draining from her body, she grasped the chair arm for support.

Anna continued 'You lost your fight two weeks ago. You went so peacefully in your sleep, the day of the consultation.'

A feeling of dread washed over Meg. She realised that everyone thought she was dead. How could they think this? she asked with herself.

She answered 'No, I am here gran, look I am alive! We need to tell everyone they have made a mistake – I am alive, not dead, look it is me!'

Her gran whispered, 'no my dear, look.' She gently pointed at the sympathy cards that engulfed the mantelpiece. 'We had your funeral a few days ago. You are gone, my love.'

Meg almost screeched. 'No that's absurd. I have only been gone three days. I have just survived that hell-hole of a ship. I was kidnapped, they made me go on the cruise – but I escaped. They faked my death, look I am here now.'

She lifted her hand to place it on her grans arm. As she did so she realised she was not able to touch her gran physically. She tried again but it was as though Megs own hand did not belong to her body.

Anna continued. 'Oh Meg, you were so strong. Alas going on your final little journey was your way of fighting your own death, don't you see that? Let go now, Meg. It is all fine. Your parents are there waiting for you. Be at peace now.'

As the reality set in, Megs legs crumbled. She let go of the chair-arm and she fell to the floor and, as she did so, her gaze flowed upwards. She was vaguely aware of something falling from her pocket but much too upset to care what it was. She lay back on the floor, her gran standing over her. She could see the love and affection in her gran's eyes, and this was her last vision. Megs gaze turned upwards, towards the heavens and at last, she knew she needed to be at peace. It was time.

Then nothingness.

Anna stood there for a few more minutes, beholding the fading vision in front of her, tears spilling down her cheeks. It was then that she noticed something on the floor. She went over and picked it up. It was a cream plastic card. As she examined it closely, she noticed it had beautiful gold edging all around it and upon further inspection, she noticed in the right-hand corner there was a little gold emblem. The emblem of a ship and the number 311 etched on it. She stared at it, before grasping it close to her heart.

'Oh Meg, my love.' she murmured before walking over to the mantlepiece and putting it at the side of the cards.

Just for safekeeping....

About the author

I am 60 years old, and I was born in Sheffield, South Yorkshire. I am married and have two children who are both just entering their forties. I live in the lovely village of Thorpe Hesley. I am a qualified tutor and have a degree in teaching and I have been working in the education sector for over 20 years. My work background is in the health and social care sector.

I have always loved reading and writing all of my life. All through my school years I have been praised and won various recognition and prizes for my writing. At seven years old, while at primary school I won a book (which I still have) as prize for the best written account of a school trip. I have a vivid imagination and have really creative dreams, there are lots of times when I have woken up and thought to myself that would make a great book!

I have a strong Yorkshire accent. On occasions, when I am writing I do write as I speak. Many times, I have had to correct my words as they get written in Yorkshire slang and some readers may not understand, so I have to take extra care! This book I have written was penned in the covid years.

Coming very soon
from the same author

Miriam's Shawl. This is a heartwarming story of wartime diary, three strong women and a family secret, that if unearthed could change all of their lives forever. Here's a snippet from it;

   'Well, my little red diary this is the first time I am writing in you, and you are such a lovely present for a girls sixteenth birthday from my ma and pa. I will treasure you forever. Today has been the best day of my life. Ever. My sixteenth birthday. Grandmother bought me a fountain pen. We had a big block of cheese for tea which tasted delicious with ma's home baked bread followed by my lovely home baked birthday cake. Afterwards I sneaked some out of the house for my love. Bill and I went up Winnard Hill with Bruno my loyal dog. We sat at the very top and felt the wind in our faces. He wished me a happy birthday and he too, gave me a present. A necklace made from delicate pink and cream seashells. He held it close to my neck and gently fastened the clasp and we both admired it. It was beautiful. He kissed me and I enjoyed it. He told me he loved me. I told him I had loved him for a very long time. We lay together, two hearts, two lovers entwined. The day I have become a full woman. It was perfect. Myperfect day.'

Double Deception. A romantic tale of learning to love, lust, deceitfulness and betrayal. Again, here is a teaser from it;

'She smiled weakly at him suddenly noticing the grandfather clock in the corner, its pendulum swaying elegantly, she tried to concentrate on this and calm herself with the movement of the clock, trying to focus on the harmonics and the pulsating ticking of the clock. This did not work. She realised the pulsating was her own heart, trying its best to escape through her ribcage. Nervously she began rummaging through her briefcase, her fingers failing to work properly for some, unknown reason. The papers slipped from her grasp and ended up all over the polished oak floor.

'Here let me help.' he said, bending his large frame over to help pick them up. As she looked up, his eyes were gazing deep into hers, only inches away. Small vibrations flickered through every part of Kristen's body.'

Keep a look out on my author page for the release dates.